Anonymous

Arthur Mason Knapp

1839-1898 - a memorial

Anonymous

Arthur Mason Knapp
1839-1898 - a memorial

ISBN/EAN: 9783337093907

Printed in Europe, USA, Canada, Australia, Japan

Cover: Foto ©Andreas Hilbeck / pixelio.de

More available books at **www.hansebooks.com**

ARTHUR MASON KNAPP

1839 - 1898

𝔄 𝔐emorial

" . . . that best portion of a good man's life,
His little, nameless, unremembered acts
Of kindness and of love."

BOSTON, MASS.
1899

ARTHUR MASON KNAPP was born August 8, 1839, at Saint Johnsbury, Vt., a place then, as now, remarkable among New England villages for the high moral and intellectual tone of its inhabitants, and as the seat not only of an important business enterprise but of an excellent institution of learning. It was in an ideal and an idyllic environment that the active mind and sensitive nature of the boy found happy and normal development. Though he removed with his parents to Boston when he was fifteen years old, he cherished a very warm affection for his native place, and a just pride in it, as long as he lived. No vacation was complete that was not prefaced or supplemented by a visit to the haunts of his boyhood.

Of his ancestry much might be

said, for one of the recreations of
his later years was an exhaustive
study of the genealogy of his family,
the result of which is a monument
of the patience and thoroughness
which marked all his investigations,
whether for himself or for others. It
is enough here to say that he was of
the seventh generation in descent
from William Knapp, who came from
England to this country, probably
with Sir Richard Saltonstall, in 1630,
and became one of the first settlers
of Watertown, Mass.; and that his
parents were Hiram and Sophronia
(Brown) Knapp.

A thoughtful, studious boy, it was
a matter of course that, on remov-
ing to Boston, Arthur should continue the line of study begun in the
St. Johnsbury Academy, and he was
at once placed in the Boston Latin
School, then under the head-master-
ship of Francis Gardner, to whom
he doubtless owed, in some measure,
the habit of accuracy, the love of
research, and the enthusiasm for

knowledge which were of such service to him and to the public in later years. Here he was graduated in 1859, at the head of a class in which there was a large number of good scholars, having borne off year after year prizes for "exemplary conduct and punctuality," for "excellence in the classical department," for "translations into Latin verse," and a Franklin medal. One of his classmates writes : —

"I well recall the Latin School — the room just as it looked in my boyhood, and the faces of the boys — Arthur usually at the head of the class. Arthur was the boy who could not be floored anywhere in that Latin Grammar. Several of us knew it well, but he knew every word of it."

And another, who was his chief competitor, adds to similar testimony, that Arthur held his leadership with such unassuming modesty as never to excite a feeling of jealousy among his classmates.

He entered Harvard College without conditions — a record which was at that time a mark of distinction — and was graduated with honor in 1863. His preference was for the classical and the scientific studies, but with characteristic fidelity he neglected none, and this was before the day of *electives*.

Though he missed somewhat of the social life of college by residing in Boston during his entire course, walking to and from Cambridge every day, he made some warm and lasting friendships, and maintained through life a loyal interest in his alma mater, from which he held the degree of A.M. as well as that of A.B. He often spoke with pride of the record made by his class since graduation, referring not only to those who, like John Fiske, Governor Greenhalge, Secretary Fairchild, Frederick Brooks, and others, have been leaders of thought and action, but to the entire membership, which, almost without exception, is composed of men of high principles and useful lives.

In September following his graduation Mr. Knapp began teaching in the classical department of Phillips Academy, Andover, under Dr. Samuel H. Taylor; but in May he was obliged to relinquish this position on account of a sudden and painful lameness, to which he was henceforth subject, at longer or shorter intervals, for the rest of his life. While still on crutches he went as private tutor of one of his Andover boys, to Irvington on the Hudson, where he remained nearly a year. In June, 1865, he was appointed sub-master of the Brookline High School, a position which, with the exception of a few months in 1865–66, during which he served as usher in the Boston Latin School, he held for ten years.

Mr. Knapp had in a marked degree many of the qualities essential to a successful teacher. A genuine sympathy with his pupils, not only in their work but in their pleasures, won their affection, while the extent and accuracy of his knowledge commanded their respect. He was companion and friend as well as teacher, and many of his former pupils, whom he always spoke of as his " boys " and " girls," could testify to his life-long interest in them. Those were happy years which he spent in teaching — years of growth, too, for he was ever a pupil with his pupils, learning while he taught.

But Mr. Knapp was to find a larger field for the exercise of his powers. From earliest boyhood he had evinced an extraordinary love of books, delighting not only in their contents but in their covers and title-pages. A remarkable memory, too, he had for what he read, and he very early formed the habit of associating ideas and classifying facts, filling his books with clippings and marginal notes, to which he turned with readiness and satisfaction for information or confirmation upon any subject under discussion in the family circle. His school and college work, as well as his teaching, had been characterized by love of research, accuracy of scholarship, and great painstaking in the search for truth, while his retentive memory had made of his mind a well-ordered storehouse of knowledge. These and other tastes and habits of mind developed by education and strengthened by experience, rendered his appointment to the service of the Boston Public Library particularly fortunate both for himself and the public.

It was on January 23, 1875, that Mr. Knapp entered upon the work which was to occupy him for the remainder of his life. For twenty-four years he gave heart and soul to the interests of the Library and the public, to which he sought to make its treasures in the largest sense available.

His first appointment was as Curator of Periodicals and Pamphlets, and of the Prince and Barton Libraries, which latter he, in collaboration with another library officer, catalogued; but for the last twenty years he held the more responsible position of Custodian of Bates Hall. To the fidelity with which he discharged the duties of this office there was abundant testimony on the occasion of his death, in notices of the press, not only of Boston but of many other cities; in official Library notices, and the funeral address of one of the Trustees; and in innumerable expressions of a sense of loss on the part of the patrons of the Library, who make grateful reference to his "ready helpfulness," his "perfect courtesy," his "unvarying kindness," his "extraordinary intelligence."

An article on the Boston Public Library, by Edmund J. Carpenter, in the *New England Magazine* of August, 1895, contains the following reference to him: —

"Mr. Arthur Mason Knapp is the librarian in charge of Bates Hall, which position he has occupied since

1878. His service with the library, however, dates from 1875; the removal of the library to the new building, in January of the present year, marked the exact completion of his twentieth year of service. With Mr. Knapp in the library there is little need of a catalogue. The searcher for information concerning any subject which he desires to study has but to apply to him and the material wished is immediately set before him. To the student whose time is precious, or who is but slightly acquainted with the system of the library, Mr. Knapp's aid is invaluable. To procure a new librarian would be an easy task compared with that of endeavoring to supply the place of such public servants as Mr. Whitney and Mr. Knapp."

To those who knew Mr. Knapp thus professionally, as well as to all who knew him personally, it was obvious that there was nothing perfunctory in his service. He loved his work. It was a personal pleasure to him to direct students and readers to the sources of knowledge, and to place before them the treasures in his keeping. He especially enjoyed solving the literary problems which were continually submitted to him, and the zest with which he followed, sometimes for weeks, a difficult quest, and his exultation when at last he "struck" some elusive fact, often reminded one of the huntsman's delight in the chase. Nothing could have been more congenial than the atmosphere of books and study in which he lived, or more agreeable than his relations with the immense constituency of readers whom he served, and with his associates in the work.

On July 2, 1873, Mr. Knapp married Miss Abbie Bartlett, daughter of James Bartlett, of Brookline, Mass. Intimately associated as fellow-teachers, as they had been, and endowed with similar tastes, while yet admirably supplementing each

other, their mutual attraction was
most natural ; and the strength and
sweetness of her character, the
brightness and quickness of her
mind, together with her charming
personality, rendered their union one
of exceptional promise. It was indeed a happy one, but, alas ! of short
duration, for she died January 26,
1876. The death of his infant son
at the same time was not only a severe blow to his affections but a bit-
ter disappointment to his hope of
perpetuating the family name and
traditions. In the shadow of this
double sorrow he walked to the end
of his days — and yet not morosely
or selfishly. He could rejoice in the
joy of others, though special instances of domestic happiness often
caused him a pang. He could look
and listen with interest when fellow-
travelers showed him photographs of
their families and discoursed upon
them with affectionate pride, and
only to his nearest betray the heart-
ache that it gave him, adding bravely

to an expression of his keen sense of loss, "But I must bear it patiently, if I can."

He did bear it patiently — cheerfully, even, and found genuine happiness in serving others, and especially in the home which he shared with his mother and sister, and from which he had been absent only during his brief married life — for while in Brookline as well as in college, he had resided with his parents, in Boston.

What he was to that home as son and brother may not here be told, but only those who knew him there knew him at his best. One who often sat at his table and by his fireside writes : —

"No one could see him in the freedom and genial fellowship of his home life without being impressed with his gentle, affectionate manner, his generous consideration of others, his sincerity and warmth of heart ; which, added to a wealth of information and a readiness to add his word of knowledge on almost any subject, together with a delicate humor that often irradiated his conversation, made him a most enjoyable companion. His knowledge never made him condescending, nor did his own literary tastes cause him to despise or disregard the tastes of others. He was the most companionable of men.

"These qualities, which characterized him always and everywhere, were most conspicuous in his own home, among his own books, in the society of his friends and his family."

Another writes : —

"I have never known a more devoted son, a more affectionate brother, or a kinder friend."

An old family servant writes : —

"I shall always thank God that I had the privilege of being Mr. Knapp's humble servant for eleven years. In all those years I never saw a frown on his face. He was always pleasant and good and kind, and I have felt ever since I left him that I had a friend to go to if I was in need."

Though he greatly valued his friends, Mr. Knapp shrank from general society, and a natural reserve veiled from strangers his peculiarly frank and sunny nature. Unconventional in his tastes and with the heart of a boy, he was content with simple pleasures and was happiest in the quiet joys of home. Vacation letters telling of keen enjoyment contain such expressions as these : —

"And yet, as always when away from you, I am eager to have my vacation over, that I may return to my loved ones."

Again : —

"My vacation has been a very pleasant one, but I am willing to go back to my work and to my own folks. People here are very kind and courteous, but none of them belong to me."

But Mr. Knapp had many resources of diversion in his quiet home life. Reading was of course the principal one. This was both a pastime and a business, for he sought not only to keep abreast, as far as possible, with the reading public, but to know what was going on in the world at large, as well as in the literary world. He had the art of reading rapidly without reading superficially, and in addition to weightier matters found time for a good deal of biography, travel and fiction. He never lost his enjoyment of the Greek and Latin classics, and in his last years many times read through his Anabasis and Cæsar as a morning recreation, without once having occasion to consult the dictionary. Of modern languages he read easily German and French, and had some knowledge of Spanish.

He always had at hand for his spare hours some special study, as that of genealogy, or of coins, in which he found relaxation and pleasure. He was skillful in the use of carpenters' tools and enjoyed contributing thereby to the comfort and convenience of the household. He loved the book-stores, and often for his afternoon outing simply exchanged the library for the bookstall. Among these and the curioshops he spent the most of what he called his "cigar money." He kept pace with the growth of the Art Museum, to which he was for many years a subscriber, and no one rejoiced more than he at every generous gift made to that institution.

His love of nature, of which he was keenly observant, contributed much to his enjoyment of life. He was in the habit of taking long walks in the suburbs and parks of Boston, where he was quick to note the varying aspects of tree and shrub, while he appreciated with an artist's eye the beauties of the landscape.

His vacations were passed mostly among the mountains of New Hampshire, to which he returned year after year with ever fresh delight, greeting familiar scenes like old friends, and repeating favorite walks with all the enthusiasm of a first visit. Many will long remember him as a delightful companion and guide over the hills and by the river, in West Campton and, earlier, in Gorham, N. H., where he spent many happy summers.

His first visit to the White Mountains was in 1862, when, with two of his classmates, he made a pedestrian tour from Boston, via Concord and Lake Winnepesaukee, to the summit of Mt. Washington, including all the principal places of interest in that region. A complete diary of the trip, contained in home letters, reads often like a record of toil and hardship, but to him it was an experience of keen enjoyment, the discomforts of which only piqued his love of adventure.

Mr. Knapp made two visits to Europe, the first in 1874, when, accompanied by his wife and his sister, he followed in general the route of the summer tourist in England and on the continent, having first enjoyed some glimpses of Ireland and Wales and more than a glimpse of Scotland. This was an experience of almost unalloyed pleasure, for which his reading and study had amply prepared him. Familiar with the historical and legendary and the literary associations of places visited, and with an appreciative eye for the beauty and grandeur of scenery, he looked at things also practically and could always give facts and figures, as well as impressions, regarding them. In view of the fact that he had as yet no thought of engaging in library work, it is interesting to note, in the home letters which form a complete diary of his travels, his interest in the manuscripts and rare editions of the British Museum, the Bodleian, and other Libraries, and his persistent efforts on several occasions to see some treasure of this sort not accessible to the general public. He studied people as well as things, and noted national and individual characteristics. Nothing escaped his keen and quick observation.

In 1880 Mr. Knapp made a second

visit to England, and though he sadly missed the companionship which had enhanced every enjoyment of the former visit, he was more than ever impressed with the natural beauty of the "snug little island"; with the magnificence of its cathedrals, of which he made a thorough study; and with the vast resources of its libraries, where he now received courtesies and privileges due a professional librarian.

Although he had not traveled extensively, Mr. Knapp was so well informed in regard to foreign countries that he sometimes gave the impression of having visited those which he knew only through books. He was especially interested in Japan, and a visit to that country was among his unfulfilled dreams. For he looked forward to a period, not of idleness nor of selfishness, either of which would have been impossible to him, but of comparative leisure, in which he might more freely indulge various quiet tastes and command more than a summer vacation for travel.

He was in the enjoyment of his usual health, when, on the ninth of December, he felt the first almost imperceptible touch of paralysis. Not recognizing it as such, however, he remained at his post the next day — a busy Saturday — though suffering greatly from the progress of the disease, which in a few days took complete possession of the left side of the body, mercifully leaving untouched the noble mind. The painful, though brief, illness was borne with patience and fortitude, and the gentle spirit was released from the body on the twenty-seventh of December, 1898.

It was not an eventful life here briefly sketched, but it embraced the deepest experiences of joy and of sorrow, and covered tranquil years of cheerful service. It made little noise in the world, but like a broad, beneficent stream, it blessed and brightened all it touched.

There was in Mr. Knapp a rare blending of gentleness and strength. He could be stern in his denunciation of wrong, and he hated all sham and cant and insincerity ; but he had such mastery of himself that he could suppress the strongest emotions, and his good-nature seemed absolutely imperturbable. His manner was always quiet ; his voice, so expressive of himself, was invariably pleasant and kindly.

He was a man whom to know once was to know always, for he was true to himself — to his principles and his sentiments. Nothing could make him swerve from what he believed to be the path of duty. Neither time nor absence had power over his friendships. Friends who met him after years of separation and silence were greeted with as much warmth and familiarity as if there had been no interruption of intercourse. He loved old friends, familiar scenes, the home of his boyhood, the city of his adoption, his country. In everything he was loyal and true.

Of his religious life, as of all deep experiences, he said little; but he was a devout and reverent believer in the simple gospel, and his life was conscientiously ordered by its precepts. Tolerant as he was of all sorts of fads, he had little patience with those who seek to substitute something else for the Christian religion. He was for many years a loyal member of the Shawmut Congregational Church, serving it quietly, but with warm heart and generous hand. He was interested in all organizations and enterprises that have for their object the amelioration of mankind, and, according to his means, contributed to their support. Many a young man is largely indebted to him for his education.

Much more might be said, but this tribute of a sister's affection is written as under the eye of one whose modesty sought to conceal his virtues.   K. K.

Some extracts from home letters will illustrate characteristics mentioned, and still further reveal the man and his way of looking at things.

The first are from the boyish diary of the pedestrian tour referred to.

'July 21. Finding a good-looking barn we asked permission to sleep there [the first night out] and were allowed to do so. We had hardly taken our knapsacks off when we were surrounded with boys and girls collected from the neighborhood. We amused them at first with the spy-glass, and when it was too dark for that we performed some very simple gymnastic feats. At every one they were completely dumbfounded and would exclaim, "I tell you that takes muscle!" "That is as good as a circus!" etc. We got so thoroughly into their good graces that they offered us pillows and quilts, but of course we declined with thanks. After they had gone we had a good laugh, for what we did was very simple, and all the apparatus we had was a pole, so that we could only turn somersaults and do a very few things. Two of the boys held the pole on their shoulders while we turned. I rather think they were a little lame the next morning. At a little before nine we spread the tent on the hay, wrapped our shawls around us and went to sleep. Twenty-three miles to-day.'

'July 26. Spent the night in a barn and started early in the morning and after walking four or five miles began to look out for breakfast. Stopped at several places but were unable to find any one who could accommodate us. At last we called at a pleasant house near a large pond and were told we could have such as they had. It was Saturday and they were rather poorly off, they said. We had cold lamb (very nice), bread and milk with splendid blueberries, *white* strawberries fresh from the vines, three kinds of pie, cake and cheese, water and cider — all for twelve cents apiece! Then we took a row of an hour on the pond and amused ourselves till the sun got too warm, when we went up to the top of a high hill and lay down and snoozed. Spent an hour and a half looking at the splendid view of Squam Lake and vicinity, eating berries and oiling our shoes. Walked along very leisurely as it was too warm for fast walking. Took a bath in a small stream to cool off. Stopped for dinner at the house of a man who preaches Sundays and cobbles week days. We slept a while under some trees and then pushed on past some very high mountains. Reached Campton Hollow at about 8 P.M., and applied at a large house for Sunday board. We have made it a plan to apply at large nice houses, for they are apt to be neater and the people are more willing to accommodate. We were received here after some hesitation.'

'July 28. We had about the pleasantest time at Dr. Sanborn's I

ever had. The family were so pleasant and obliging, and when we came
to settle they refused point blank to
accept anything. They said they did
not keep a tavern and hardly ever
entertained strangers, but for some
reason or other — they knew not
why — they received us. We bade
them good-by last night, but found
this morning that they were up and
had a hot breakfast for us, and that
the doctor was intending to give us a
lift in his wagon. Mrs. S. gave us
a pan of cookies to eat among the
mountains, as they would taste good,
she said, and a large bundle of sand-
wiches to eat during the day. The
doctor carried us up to the borders
of Woodstock, ten miles on our way.
He took us through the pleasantest
scenery he could find, fording the
Pemigewasset and riding along in
the bed of the stream, which was
only five or six inches deep.

'After beginning our walk we kept
on for two or three miles until we
came to a brook, where we bathed

and also washed some clothes. The brook was a perfect jewel, full of little waterfalls and looked as if it had some trout in it. After that we walked on a mile or two and then stopped to rest, for it was awfully hot. Got dinner and walked a few rods, till we came to a little church, in the shadow of which we are now resting, waiting for it to get a little cooler. We are only four and a half miles from the Flume House and in the midst of very lofty mountains and splendid scenery. We are enjoying ourselves very much now, better than during the first part of the trip, when we were so sore and lame. We can see the Franconia Notch very plainly from this spot where we are resting.'

'July 30. My last letter was written on the top of a high hill near Bethlehem, and now we are twenty-three miles from that place. We walked to a farmer's a little this side of Bethlehem and took supper and found a barn to sleep in. I never slept better in my life than I did there on the hay, not waking once from the time when I lay down till this morning at half past four o'clock. Marched seven miles before breakfast, then got our bread and milk. After breakfast we walked on till we came to a good place for bathing. We have bathed in the Sowhegan, at its junction with the Merrimac, in Lake Winnepesaukee, the Ammonoosuc, and a great many small streams. We had hardly started on our way when we were overtaken by a very severe thunderstorm. We walked on, hoping to find some shelter, till we reached the White Mountain House, where we took dinner. While we were here the Mr. B., whom I mentioned in my last letter, drove up in great style, with four horses, two servant men, etc. He spoke very pleasantly to us and said we might meet again.

'We started for Crawford's at 1.45 and just after we had passed Giant's Grave another tremendous storm came up and we were obliged to walk four miles in as hard a rain as I ever saw, with mud almost over our shoes. When we reached Crawford's we found Mr. B.'s party and one or two others whom we had seen before at the Profile House, and we were immediately the lions of the day, and were surrounded by ladies, gentlemen, and children, and questioned and wondered at to our hearts' content.'

'July 31. Started at about 8 A.M. for Mt. Washington and reached the Tip-Top House at 2 P.M. after nearly six hours' climb. I never saw such traveling, the ascents sometimes being as steep as the roof of a house, and over loose rocks, so that we had to jump from one to another, which was very fatiguing, and my strength was not as great as usual.[1] About two hours from the summit it began to rain hard, and we could not hold umbrellas, for the wind blew a perfect hurricane. We were all of us

---

[1] He had been ill the day before.

soaked through and through. When we reached the Tip-Top House I was so used up that I sat down on the floor and almost dropped asleep. A gentleman saw how badly off I was and guided me to the Summit House, where beds could be had. I called for a room, had myself rubbed dry, changed my clothes completely and lay down. I fell asleep immediately but slept only a few minutes. I felt better when I awoke and after a hearty dinner felt perfectly well. The rain cleared off towards night and gave us a splendid sunset and a very good view. There were four of us Harvard boys there and a gentleman with his daughter. We had the Summit House to ourselves and enjoyed the evening very much, sitting around the fire. The house is a real snug little place, with very small rooms just large enough for a bed and a passage along the front side of it. The partitions are of cloth, so that every word which is spoken in any room can be distinctly heard.

The beds looked quite neat, but when I turned down the clothes I found that they had not been well aired, and so we slept on the outside with our shawls around us. I never passed a more quiet or comfortable night in my life. Up at half past four to see the sun rise and were so fortunate as to find the morning clear. At 4.45 the sun appeared and gave us a most gorgeous sight. There were clouds far below us, upon which the rays of the sun struck and tinged them with a rosy light. The clouds were magnificent, like a great white sea, with here and there a dark green mountain top projecting. We could see the Green Mountains distinctly, and a mist or cloud where the ocean lay.

'At about 7.30 A.M. six of us, including Mr. W. and his daughter, started with a guide for Tuckerman's Ravine, a deep gorge between Mt. Washington and Mt. Franklin. After an hour's scramble over the rocks, down the channels of brooks, over numberless difficulties, we reached the bottom. Here we found an enormous amount of snow and enjoyed ourselves snowballing, sliding on the snow, etc. There is an arch through the snow three hundred feet long and wide enough for several persons to go abreast. The snow is thirty or forty feet deep above the arch. I found several kinds of flowers growing near the snow and some Greenland plants, and made quite a collection, but have given them away to two ladies here who are very much interested in botany and had a great desire to possess them. We scrambled back over the rocks and reached the top at about eleven o'clock. [Here follows an appreciative account of the "pluck" of the young lady of the party.] Took dinner and started down the carriage road for the Glen. Saw lots of people who had seen us before. They would come up and say, "Ah, here are the travelers we have met so often!" and would begin conversing with us as pleasantly as if we had been clothed in purple and fine linen. We walked down to the Glen House in less than three hours. The road is a splendid triumph of engineering, not at all steep, rising one foot in eight and a half, very wide, sloping inwards, and with a high wall round the outside. At the Glen House we met a party which we had met at Crawford's and at the Tip-Top House, and also a classmate of ours. Started for North Conway in the afternoon and visited Crystal and Glen Ellis Falls on our way, by far the finest falls I ever saw. Walked seven miles without seeing a house and did not see even a clearing till 8.30 P.M., when we came upon a party of eleven fellows encamped in front of a house. All but three were students of Brown University. They had a team to carry their baggage, a large tent to sleep in, and everything necessary for a good time. They invited us to spend the night with them and we did so. . . . In the morning started at a little past five and walked till we came to a place to bathe. Took breakfast at Jackson and reached North Conway at 11.30, having walked thirteen miles. Here I found Sister and was n't I glad to see her! I had not heard a word from home since I left Concord, where I found a letter from George.'

The diary closes with the record of a solitary march of forty-four miles on a hot day, the party having broken up at North Conway, where he spent a few days.

The following selections are from letters written during his first European tour: —

'EDINBORO, July 1, 1874.

'This morning we started at 10.15 for Melrose and Abbotsford. On the way we passed Crichton and Borthwick Castles, both in ruins, the latter mentioned by Scott in Marmion. At Melrose we spent about an hour examining the ruins of the Abbey. I was prepared for disappointment, but was delighted with everything we saw. The capitals and carved work are exquisite, far beyond anything we have seen before. The ornaments are not eaten away by the tooth of time, but seem as sharply edged as at first. Such numbers of figures expressing everything possible to be expressed in stone — grotesque faces, distorted bodies, saints and demons, apostles and kings, a perfect museum of carving. We saw the tombs of Alexander II and his queen Joanna, the wizard Michael Scott, James Douglas, killed in the famous Chevy Chase in 1388, and others of the same line, the spot where the heart of Robert Bruce was buried, the grave of Tom Purdie, the faithful forester of Walter Scott.

'We then rode about three miles to Abbotsford, where we were raced through the apartments open to the public, glancing at portraits of Scott, his mother, wife, son, and daughters, of James IV and VI, Cromwell,

Dryden, Thomson, Queen Elizabeth and Mary, of the Duchess of Buccleuch, to whom the Last Minstrel tells his Lay, and others that I now fail to recall ; at interesting objects, such as guns belonging to Rob Roy, Andreas Hofer, and Scott ; swords of his son and of the Marquis of Montrose, execution swords, a two-handed sword from Bosworth Field, and one from Culloden ; armor and weapons of all kinds from all lands and times ; Mary Queen of Scots' seal, and a painting of her head in a charger ; lots of beautiful and rare mementoes ; gifts from illustrious persons of different lands ; carved and inlaid furniture four or five centuries old. I could have spent hours there instead of a few minutes. We then drove to Dryburgh Abbey, where we saw the tomb of Scott and those of his son, his wife, his daughter, and Lockhart. Mrs. Lockhart is buried in London. Scott's great-granddaughter, his only descendant, is to be married next month (or this) to a Mr. Maxwell, who takes the name of Scott and resides at Abbotsford, which, after the fifteenth of this month, is to be closed to the public. It seemed hard that a man like Scott, who had worked so long and faithfully, should not be allowed to live longer to enjoy the fruits of his toil.

'We took train at St. Boswell's and returned home. Our usual good fortune attended us — the weather was just right and all our plans prospered. Just before we entered our hotel the rain began to fall and it continued for some time.'

'LONDON, July 24, 1874.

'To-day we have spent at the British Museum, hard at work seeing an infinite number of interesting things. We first visited the gallery of Roman statues. I was interested in the busts of the emperors and the old classic writers so familiar to me.

In this department were splendid mosaics, some containing admirable human faces, as fine in color and outline as a painting — one face as much as five feet in height.

'We then examined the Elgin marbles, among which we saw the frieze of the Parthenon, statues by Phidias, immense fragments from the Mausoleum of Mausolus. You can form some idea of the statues of that structure from the fact that my hand out flat would not cover one toe of a woman's foot we saw.

'In the Egyptian Hall we saw a granite fist as large as a hogshead; the *head* of Rameses II, nine feet high; a sarcophagus supposed to have once contained the body of Alexander the Great; the Rosetta Stone, the key to the hieroglyphics; multitudes of statues, monuments, etc. We also saw in another room an Egyptian wig; the bones of Mycerinus, who lived a hundred years before Abraham; together with an immense number of smaller objects like those in the Way collection in Boston.

'We passed through rooms containing Assyrian antiquities, colossal statues of human-headed lions and bulls; Egyptian papyri in wonderful preservation; vases of all sizes and shapes; bronzes; Greek and Roman armor; bells from the early shrines and churches of Ireland (one from that of St. Senan, who died in 554); glass from the earliest period up; ancient British and Saxon relics. The gem room, to which we were admitted, contained the famous Portland Vase, thousands of the most wonderful cameos and gems, specimens of jewelry from Nineveh, Babylon, Etruria, and other ancient lands, coins, rings, etc. One cameo head of Augustus is said to be worth three thousand guineas. The Blacas collection (a small part of the contents of the room) cost forty-eight thousand pounds.

'In the Library we saw first editions of Shakespeare, Milton, Dante,

Don Quixote, Walton, Robinson Crusoe, Common Prayer; the book that gave Henry VIII the title of Defender of the Faith; the first printed copy of the Psalter, 1457; first book with a date; first Greek classic printed; first printed Virgil, 1501; Horace, printed from the smallest type ever made; first Chaucer, 1476 (Caxton); Fifteen O's and Other Prayers, 1490 (Caxton); The Game and Playe of the Chesse, 1474 (Caxton); the first book ever printed in England; the first Bible ever printed, 1450 (a defective copy sold at auction lately for thirty-four hundred guineas); the Mazarin Bible, 1455; old charters by Ethelred, Edgar, Canute, Edward the Confessor, Henry I, Richard I, Odo of France, and many other kings or dignitaries; Codex Alexandrinus, fifth century; Genesis and Exodus, 464; Bible written by command of Charlemagne, 796–800; Jewish roll of the Pentateuch, fourteenth century; many of the most elegantly bound books and manuscripts, the covers in some instances being set with jewels.'

The next day after describing a number of historic localities visited, he says : —

'We then walked up to the British Museum, for I was bound to see Shakespeare's autograph, which we were unable to see yesterday. By dint of inquiry and persistency we succeeded in seeing that and the original Magna Charta, which is not usually shown. The latter was nearly destroyed in a fire many years ago, but was carefully flattened out and placed under glass. The seal was an irregular mass of wax. We also saw another copy made at the same time but not signed by the king.

'One of the attendants gave me a pass to the Reading Room, an immense dome 140 feet in diameter, larger than that of St. Peter's at Rome, though not nearly so high. Having satisfied our curiosity here, we walked home well pleased with our day's work.'

'SALISBURY, July 30, 1874.

'Immediately after breakfast we had a barouche and span ready and started for Stonehenge. Soon we passed Old Sarum, so famous as a British, Roman, Saxon, and English stronghold, and often referred to in the great Reform struggle of 1832, as it could send members to Parliament although having no inhabitants. Alfred the Great built part of the fortifications in 871 and soon after fought a great battle with the Danes near by. The appearance of the ruins is very striking, being quite a high hill, the sides artificially graded.

'After riding a few miles we came to Salisbury Plain, over which we drove, the turf being so smooth and soft that the wheels made no noise, and the ground so level that one could drive in any direction perfectly well. This country is chalk formation, and everywhere scattered through the chalk are flint nodules of all sizes up to half as large as my head. These often are of fantastic shapes, like bones, and when scattered along singly or in small heaps give a very strange, graveyard appearance to the country. There were great numbers of little blue bells thick with blossom, like the bull-thistle, but not on a stalk, small white convolvuli, and many other flowers. Here and there we saw fairy rings, of all sizes, sometimes single circles, sometimes intertwined. I always supposed one must use considerable imagination in distinguishing between the ring and the surrounding grass, but here the contrast was as marked as between green grass and ripe oats. I had often read of such phenomena in Scott's poems, but had never seen them before. As we approached our destination we passed many tumuli, supposed to be ancient graves, some standing alone fifteen or twenty feet high and one or two hundred feet in circumference, others surrounded by a ditch forming a perfect circle.

'We could see the Druidical stones long before we reached them. You can form no idea of the strange impressiveness of these old monuments — no habitation near, only a vast plain with here and there a shepherd with his flock, or a startled hare running swiftly away. The stones are enormous, far surpassing my expectations. I had seen the size stated in books, but figures could give no idea of their vastness.

'After spending about an hour here we started on our return, by another route which took us along the valley of the Avon, through a most lovely region. The air was filled with the song of larks, which were as common as sparrows and robins with us. Now and then one would rise far up into the clouds and then suddenly drop to the earth. I had never seen a lark before, and was delighted to see them so abundant and so tame, for they did not seem alarmed by the carriage, but kept on singing even when we were very near. Some of the farmhouses with thatched roofs and fresh green hedges and immense elms seemed like the pictures of English homes I have often seen. In one wall I noticed splendid fossils, ammonites, a foot or more in diameter. Just before reaching home we passed the site of the old Royal Tournament ground, one of the five places appointed in the time of Richard I for such exercise.

'Immediately after our arrival at the hotel we walked up to the Close, which includes many houses, the Bishop's Palace with its gardens of several acres, and a very extensive green about the cathedral itself. As the door was open we went into the cathedral and were taken about by the verger, who was very intelligent and satisfactory. The building is the most beautiful, and most nearly approaches my ideal of a cathedral, of any we have seen, not even excepting York and Westminster. The spire is four hundred feet high and most graceful and elegant, the carvings fresh and entire, the whole perfect. Within, repairs are in progress which, when complete, will make the interior exquisite. The Chapter House is entirely restored and resembles those of York and Westminster, particularly the latter. The cloisters are the most beautiful we have seen and in the center are two very large cedars of Lebanon.

'We afterwards strolled through the Bishop's Garden, a most charming place, where we saw some magnificent trees — among them some very large cedars of Lebanon, one at least two and a half feet in diameter. Just as we left the cathedral a hard shower came up, but it lasted only about ten minutes, when the sun came out and the greensward around the building became inexpressibly beautiful in the bright light, relieved now and then by the shadows of grand old elms.

'You may know that Old Sarum was

removed to a lower site, the present city of Salisbury, and we were interested in seeing numerous carved stones in the wall around the Close, evidently brought from the old city.

'This was our last day in England and was a most glorious finale to our stay on the snug little island.'

'Chamonix, August 13, 1874.

'Yesterday morning we started at seven o'clock from Geneva on the diligence. The road for miles ran through scenery not very unlike that of New Hampshire, the houses and villages, however, very different. As we approached the mountains, the country changed; instead of hills mountains surrounded us on every side, often we were completely shut in, precipices on all hands. We followed the valley of the Arve most of the way, often hundreds of feet above it, but so near that a slight toss would send a stone into the stream. At St. Martin's we stopped for lunch, and had directly before us the Mont

Blanc range of snow-capped summits. You can form no idea from words or pictures of the splendor of the sight. The day was one of the most perfect ever created, the sun bright and warm, and the reflection from the vast fields of snow utterly indescribable. The whiteness was such that a white envelope held up in comparison looked gray and dingy.

The road was a triumph of engineering, for miles and miles running along the sides of the mountains, with a constant and uniform ascent, cut out from the solid rock which towered above us often hundreds of feet. On the other side of the road the descent was as great. We were all on the outside of the coach and could look directly down, perhaps a thousand feet, to the Arve, flowing in its rocky channel below. In one place we went through quite a long tunnel. Towards three o'clock we entered Chamonix, where we put up at the Mont Blanc Pension. From my window I can look directly out upon Mont Blanc and half a dozen others from two to three miles high, all glittering in their robes of white. I shall not attempt description, but, as usual, make my letter a journal of my adventures and wanderings.'

From the second series of letters:

'Canterbury, June 24, 1880.

'I think you would have laughed to see me to-night at the Saracen's Head, seated at a table — before me a huge piece of roast beef from which I cut slices from time to time ; a mass of cheese a foot square ; a loaf of bread like that in the picture of the Cottager's Daughter ; a mug of beer and a cup of tea — trying my best to make up for the hardships and famine of the past twelve or thirteen days [the voyage]. . . .

'Before hunting up an inn I wandered through the streets of this quaint old city, looking with curiosity at its many ancient streets, churches, and houses. A great many of the latter have projecting stories or gable ends, entirely unlike anything in our country. Just after leaving the station I passed through the only remaining gate of the city, looking like some ancient castle, and just by it was the church of St. Dunstan, where Sir Thomas More's head is buried, resting upon the breast of his daughter Margaret. You may remember Tennyson alludes to her in his Dream of Fair Women. The story is told in the Book of Golden Deeds.

'By chance I stumbled upon this queer old inn — perhaps centuries old, and liked its appearance so well that I concluded to stay over night. The cheer placed before me, you already know. My room is up one flight, huge rough beams across the ceiling, pictures upon the walls, and handsome furniture — evidently the best room.

'June 25. I arose early and took a long walk before the rest of the household were stirring. You know the English are not famous for early rising, rarely beginning the day before nine o'clock. After wandering around through various streets, such as Mercery, where the pilgrims used to purchase offerings, indulgences, etc., I came to St. Martin's Church, which antiquaries assign to the second century. It may not be so old as that, but at least it is centuries older than the Cathedral, as its appearance plainly shows, the material of which it is built being largely Roman brick. I wish I could depict to you its beauty and make you see it as I saw it this morning. There had been rain in the night, but now the sun was shining and everything sparkling in its light. The grass and foliage seemed even greener than English green.

'The church stands on the side of St. Martin's Hill, and the approach is directly up the steep to the front, which is mainly a huge square tower covered with the greenest, glossiest ivy, the stems of which have united near the ground into a solid mass of wood at least three feet thick. The door is very small and on each side is an old yew tree. The ground around is a burying place which for its size has more beautiful monuments than any other cemetery I know of. Most of them are recumbent or in the form of old crosses with quaint carvings. I have photographs which will give you some idea of its appearance.

'I also visited Dane John, a park containing the remains of the old city walls and an artificial mound from which there is a fine view of the surrounding country, and then hurried back to my hotel, where I had a most delicious breakfast.'

'SALISBURY, June 26, 1880.

'Visitors are not allowed to enter and stroll about the Cathedral till after morning service, which lasts from ten to eleven. This late beginning of sight-seeing is a very serious inconvenience in my progress. Our party consisted of a gentleman and two ladies, who were in great haste to catch a certain train. Their haste spoiled my enjoyment, and so after they had gone I purchased a guide-book from the verger, and in consideration of this was told that I might take my time, go where I pleased, the doors of the choir and of the cloisters being left unlocked for my convenience. I was glad to accept the offer and stayed for an hour or more, viewing it thoroughly from all points, sitting down occasionally and feasting my eyes. I could hardly keep back the tears as I gazed. Nothing so beautiful, so grand, and so impressive ever met my eyes. Six years ago it was in process of restoration, all except the nave being boarded up. Now everything is perfect, clean, bright, and glorious. I don't believe there is any building on earth more beautiful in itself and its surroundings.'

'OXFORD, June 28, 1880.
'After securing a room at the Mitre and leaving my handbag, I

took my Barton Catalogue[1] and started for the Bodleian Library. Here I was received very cordially and shown through the library, through room after room of manuscripts to which the public are not admitted — thousands and thousands of volumes of manuscripts of priceless value.

'I afterwards spent some hours in strolling through the various colleges, the buildings, the quads, the walks, the parks, etc. What a paradise Magdalen College is, with its gardens, park, meadows, deer, Addison's Walk and other attractions!

'I then returned to the hotel, ate a hearty dinner, read, wrote some postal cards, and retired at about eight o'clock, strangely fatigued considering the little work I had done.'

'June 29. This morning I awoke at a very early hour, thoroughly rested, and ready for one of the most glorious days in my eventful

[1] The catalogue of the Barton Library (see p. 10), a copy of which he took as a gift to the Bodleian.

career. After what the English would call an early breakfast, I took the train for Warwick, passing through Banbury, where I bought some delicious, freshly baked Banbury cakes. At Warwick I was unable to see the castle, as the Earl was at home and would allow no one to visit even the grounds.

'I arranged with a fly (*i. e.,* carriage) to take me to Coventry and other places. We drove all about Warwick, visited St. Mary's Church and Beauchamp Chapel, saw Leicester's Hospital, and then drove down to the bridge over the Avon, whence we had a beautiful view of the castle. We then started for Coventry. You have probably heard of the two Englishmen who laid a wager as to the most beautiful walk in England. Upon comparing notes it was found that one had named the road from Coventry to Warwick, the other that from Warwick to Coventry. I agree perfectly with both.

'Imagine a broad road eight or ten

miles long, shaded on both sides with magnificent elms and oaks ; a hard, smooth roadway about twenty-five feet wide, in the center, and at one side, beneath the shadow of these huge trees, a footpath from three to six feet wide, carefully graded and graveled, and all the remaining space between the trees fresh greensward. That is the road we drove over. But more remains to tell.

'After stopping to admire Guy's Cliff, I was advised to visit Stoneleigh Abbey. This was in ancient times an abbey occupied by Cistercian monks, but seized by Henry VIII and confiscated. Much of the house is comparatively modern, in style not very unlike Chatsworth. Most of the rooms are paneled from floor to ceiling with old oak. It is a storehouse of interesting portraits and other works of art. I saw original portraits of Henry VIII and Elizabeth, both by Holbein ; of Durer, by himself ; of Byron ; and many by Vandyke and Kneller. The park is immense and every seven years is perambulated by a large party of men and boys to fix the boundaries. The circuit is over thirty and less than forty miles. Through this park we drove for several miles before we got back to our Coventry turnpike. At Kenilworth I stopped and saw the ruins of the castle. We drove all about Coventry, so that I have a very good idea of that interesting, dirty old city.

'The whole drive was perfectly glorious — with my pen I can give but a slight idea of it. The only drawback was your absence. . . . At Coventry I took cars for Rugby, where I was obliged to wait an hour for a train to Leicester. At the latter place I was forced to wait fifty minutes for a train to Nottingham. Between Nottingham and Lincoln I had a capital view of Newark Castle, where King John died in 1216.

'At Lincoln I stopped at the Great Northern Railway Hotel. Took a short walk before breakfast and after breakfast was so fortunate as to find the verger ready to show the Cathedral before the morning service. This saved me a delay of five hours in reaching Boston. The hill leading up to the Cathedral is the steepest I ever saw in any city. It is like going up stairs with stairs left out. At a little shop I happened to see a plate of old coins in the window. I went in, looked them over, and bought a lot of Roman and very old English coins, silver and copper, for a few pence apiece. Lincoln was a Roman city, and in digging sewers old coins, mosaic pavements, etc., are often found. . . . Took cars for Boston, passing in plain sight of the castle of Tattershall, erected in the fifteenth century, now in ruins, but a most imposing brick-work tower.

'At Boston I saw the old church in which John Cotton preached, and on my mentioning the letter in my charge [in the Boston Public Library] from Cotton to his wife, the verger took me up a winding stairway in one of the little towers, to a room to which the public are not admitted, and showed me the old registers of marriage signed by Cotton, and the record of Cotton's own marriage, also old manuscripts, old books worth their weight in gold, and other curious things. The registers are complete from 1558 to the present time — a very unusual circumstance. I had a very pleasant time at a little house opposite the church, where the verger lives and where I called to look at photographs which I saw exhibited in the window. The woman who waited upon me was a very pleasant, talkative person. It was market day, and such a hubbub and noise as filled the market-place, people shouting the merits of their wares, Cheap-Jacks in full blast, just as Professor Churchill represents in Dr. Marigold's Prescription, and other strange sights and sounds.'

'July 1. At Cambridge I made for Trinity College, the finest English foundation to be seen anywhere.

Upon entering the library I was told that strangers were not admitted, but when I presented my card, was told that that made all the difference in the world. The librarian was very attentive and showed me about, pointing out the rarities. It is a beautiful room, or hall, and contains a very valuable collection of books.

'I walked about a good deal, through the pleasure grounds along the Cam, the quads of different colleges, to the University Library, where my card was immediately sent to Mr. Bradshaw, the Librarian, who received me with open arms. For an hour or more I was treated with the utmost kindness, and when I left, Mr. Bradshaw accompanied me to the lower door. You see it is something to be a professional. Mr. Winsor sent me a most flattering letter of introduction to one of the officers in the British Museum, which I have not yet used.'

TRIBUTES.

From a great number of tributes, public and private, all of which were most grateful to a bereaved family, a few are selected, in order to show that in the various relations of life, as well as in his home, Mr. Knapp was honored and loved.

The funeral services, held in Shawmut Church, were conducted by the pastor, Rev. William E. Barton, D.D., assisted by Rev. James DeNormandie, D.D., representing the Trustees of the Public Library, and by Rev. S. E. Herrick, D.D., a family friend. The pall-bearers were Mr. Herbert Putnam, Mr. James L. Whitney, and Mr. Lindsay Swift, representing the Library staff; and Mr. Frank Wood, Mr. Frederic Hinckley, and Mr. W. A. Chapin, representing Shawmut Church. The large attendance of men and women from various walks in life testified to the respect and affection in which he was held.

The work of a great Public Library
can be appreciated only by those
who know something of it. You see
a large and beautiful building shel-
tering seven or eight hundred thousand volumes ; you see the ceaseless
procession of patrons ; you see the
attendants delivering to them the
books ; and you think this is all, and
that it is plain and easy. Of what is
done before the public can be served ;
of the vast and hidden details ; of
the choice and cataloguing and ar-
rangement of books ; of the years
of careful preparation ; of the co-
operation, industry, studied and unbroken attention ; of the promptness
and forbearance ; of the patience and
knowledge and alertness required to
meet the daily demands of thousands
of inquiring minds — of all this nothing is known.

The public is most exacting of its servants, and feels that all their time and strength and acquisitions belong to it without a moment's delay, without any manifestation of impatience or weariness.

To have been for nearly a quarter of a century in such a service is itself a great testimony to one's worth, and to have been for twenty years the trusted head of one of the leading departments of the Public Library is a proof of merit to which words can add very little.

The accumulated and well-arranged learning of our friend, as if it were all in a multitude of familiar drawers, was freely given to any inquirer. Many came every day to ask not only for books, but to know what books or what essays had been written upon every subject recent or ancient, plain or abstruse, that the fertile mind of man has ever thought of — and here was one who seemed to remember all ; whose good taste and good judgment were ever ready to suggest not only books, which is a very little matter, but the *best* books, which is a very important matter touching the higher questions of life. So that his daily work was to give to hundreds better ideals of human actions and human character, making his mission one with all those who in every form of teaching, in journalism, in schools, and in the church are helping this to be a better world.

What knowledge, what graciousness, what a ready and unfailing sympathy, what a sense of humor, which so lightens the annoyances of public station, what a spirit of self-denying, what faithfulness marked his daily life.

When St. Paul would express the highest merit of a steward he says, " It is required that a man be found faithful "; and when Jesus Christ would set the seal of divine favor and divine joy upon a man's work, he told the beautiful story of one who was faithful to his talents, his gifts.

Servants and stewards of the Most High, all of us, our best reward is that we be found faithful. Only faithful! In the midst of so much that is unfaithful, in the midst of so many noisy activities which count for nothing and end in nothing, God grant that when our work, like his, is done, there may be written upon it the promise of Jesus, "Thou hast been faithful over a few things, I will make thee ruler over many things, enter thou into the joy of thy Lord."

We know it cannot be otherwise, and we would not have it otherwise, but the heart has its own way of looking at the things which belong to the heart, and we are never ready for the summons which calls our loved ones away. The separation is always hard, and we miss the familiar voice and the loved form, and the lonely paths are the sad paths. The heart knows its own bitterness, and loves to dwell upon it. We see those on whom our hopes are centered, whom we have most fondly loved, drop away, and we ask, "Are the infinite purposes defeated, or are we listening only to an unfinished tale, to be told out elsewhere?" It is in the presence of death that we first and most surely believe there is no death.

What this loss is to this inner circle, privileged to be at one with him, we may not now venture to say, but they will be grateful as long as they live for this life, and they know that he will be with them still in innumerable sweet and precious memories of gentle companionship, of daily duty and sacrifice, of unfaltering devotion, of unbroken love; in influences which belong to the things which are unseen, but eternal.

It is ever the story of old; a cloud has received him out of our sight. The veil of the future is never lifted, but because it is not, we believe it has fallen around us from the same Eternal Goodness which makes this life so dear and grateful.

What to us is shadow to him is day,
  And the way he knoweth,
And not on a blind and aimless way
  The spirit goeth;

but a way which duty, faith, and love
make straight and shining to the
Eternal Home.

Address of

Rev. Wm. E. Barton, D.D.

The custom of speaking publicly of our friends when they have been taken from us is manifestly decreasing, yet it is one which I shall be sorry to see wholly given up. There are so many lives that have been little known that deserve a tribute of respect; there are so many other lives that have been such examples of conspicuous faithfulness that it seems inappropriate that they should withdraw and no friend take public note of their departure; and there are other lives whose lesson is so patent that we only need to stand a moment and say, "Faithful! He has been faithful, and God has taken him," and yet we want to say so much as that at least.

Dr. DeNormandie has spoken of the fidelity of our friend in that which he made his life work. Of that fidelity Dr. DeNormandie has known well. In this quarter of a century it was the fortune of others to know him here in this church and in the beauty of his home life. Of that home life I may not speak; he was always the model son, the model brother; there are no regrets; there is nothing to forgive. That home life was one of rare beauty and symmetry. Married for two and a half years, his infant son and his young wife were taken from him at once; and that sad event cast a shadow over all the years that he lived afterward — so sad a shadow that he rarely mentioned it, even to those who were nearest to him. Yet he lived a cheerful life, an unusually happy life. The fidelity which those recognized who knew him in his public work was characteristic of every part of his life. Indeed, I think we may say it was the key to an interpretation of his life. He was found faithful.

It is not easy for us to analyze the

character of our friends. We may
do that with strangers and those
whom we have known at a distance,
but we rarely find joy in doing it
with those who live nearest to us.
In the half a dozen years that I
knew Mr. Knapp, I think perhaps I
came to know him somewhat unusually well. I knew him, indeed, in
his work in the Library. It was an
inspiration to me, coming to this old
city, so rich in its historic and literary associations, to have him spread
out before me in the Library rare old
editions and ancient manuscripts and
parchments, about which I had read
but which I had never seen, and
some of them literally worth their
weight in gold — many of them
worth far more for the treasures
which they contained. It was a
never-ceasing inspiration to know
him in that way, a man of liberal
education and intellectual tastes.
He had read so widely and di-
gested what he knew so well, and
arranged his knowledge so as to

make it so readily available, that those who came for information, eager themselves for knowledge but many of them knowing little how they might obtain it, always found him ready. In special studies which I found time to pursue, he was my most faithful and helpful friend.

But it was in other relations that I knew him best. In this church he was a consistent, regular attendant, a member whose interest extended to the whole work and prosperity of the church. He was a man of sincere and simple faith, a man who worshiped God in the beauty of holiness. He was a man whose intellectual nature had not swallowed up his spiritual life, he was a man who in his own secret heart lived near to God. He was not an ostentatious man, and he would have been the last to wish to-day for fulsome praise. The words which are spoken of him are the simple facts about him, which are more eloquent than any studied words of careful eulogy or of extravagant praise.

He delighted in the service of God. He never sought official positions; when this church pressed upon him offices, in his modesty he shrank from them and declined them. Yet even so modest a man as he could not live in a church all these years without being known for his true worth, and those who knew and honored him here are saddened, every one, by his departure. Of him I think may be said that rare, rich thing, that all who knew him honored him, and all who knew him well loved him; and those who to-day speak these words, which are meant to be words of comfort, might, in their own thought, more fitly take their place among those who need to be comforted.

Death is the one great fact in human life to which we refuse to adjust our thought. We know that we must die; we know nothing so certain as death; yet it comes to us with a surprise. We count it an intrusion, a sort of impertinence, and we are never quite prepared for it. It seems to us an incongruity, an inconsistency; and our persistent refusal to accommodate ourselves to it, our yearning for something more, our insistence that what seems the end cannot be the end, is the highest tribute which the mind of man has ever paid to the dignity and the beauty of life and its continued desirability; and that we can suffer as we sometimes suffer in the loss of those who are taken from us is the richest tribute which God enables any human heart to place upon the bier of friendship and of love. We need the words and the hopes of the Gospel. We need to strengthen our faith with all our knowledge of the dignity and the worthiness of human life. We need the inspiration and the certitude of the Gospel of Jesus Christ, and the truth that in his resurrection, his newness of life, there is hope for all who sleep in him. In him we may learn to interpret death anew, even as we have learned already in part the larger meaning of death in the world without us.

I remember how the day died and how the sun went down and left the earth in darkness, and had I seen it only once I should have thought that that was the end; but I remember that even as the sun sank to its grave the west grew glorious with colors more splendid than those of the noontide; and even as I look and peer into the darkness, there shines about me the gray and then the red and then all the golden, glorious luster of the dawn. And I remember how the year died, how the leaves fell one by one, and were hurried along by the keen cold blast; I remember how the heavens put on their mourning robes of cloud, and wept their tears over the great dead world, and then gently covered it in its shroud of snow; and had I seen it only once I should have thought

that that must be the end. Yet
never a leaf fell from the tree but
left beneath it the bud of a larger
life ; and never a winter came but
the autumn grew glorious in all the
colors of the rainbow, which were
not painted by the utility of nature,
but grew out of the abundant hope
which is God's promise of another
year when earth shall rise from winter and live in the glory of the
spring. And so I remember how my
friend died, and slipped away when
the arms of love were not long
enough or strong enough to hold
him, and how there was borne out
from our home the sacred dust which
still looked as he had looked, and
reminded us of every gracious act and
kindly word ; and I have seen it but
a few times, and so at first it seems
to me that this is the end ; but I
comfort myself with the promise and
hope of him to whom the mysteries
of this life and the next were clear,
who himself tasted death for every
man, and who rose triumphant from

the dead, leading captivity captive, that we might say, "O death, where is thy sting? O grave, where is thy victory?" Wherefore let us comfort one another with these words of the Blessed Saviour and of those to whom he gave wisdom for our present comfort.

At a meeting of the class of 1863, of Harvard College, held on Commencement Day, June 28, 1899, the following tribute, offered by Mr. Thomas B. Peck, was adopted and placed on record: —

Arthur Mason Knapp died at his home in Boston, December 27, 1898, after a brief but painful illness, of paralysis. He had been engaged in his usual employment in the Boston Public Library up to the time of his illness, and although somewhat delicate in physique, is believed to have been usually in possession of good health. From his boyhood onward he had been remarkable for his love of literature. At the Boston Latin School, where he was prepared for college, he stood easily at the head of a class which contained a large number of good scholars. Somewhat older and therefore more mature in mind than most of his classmates, he was enabled by his industry, his clearness of mind and his remarkable memory to hold his leadership, and did so with such unassuming modesty as never to excite a feeling of jealousy among his classmates. He held a high rank for scholarship during his college course, in which he showed the same capacity and devotion to study as in his school days. His intellect was sound rather than brilliant. While he won the respect of the class by his sterling traits of character, his retiring disposition and the fact that he made his home with his parents in Boston and spent the working hours of the week only in Cambridge prevented him from becoming as well known in the class socially as would otherwise have been the case.

To an unusual degree Knapp's life was spent in a congenial atmosphere of books and study. After graduation he adopted the profession of teaching, and taught in the Phillips

Academy in Andover and in the
Brookline High School, until in January, 1875, he entered the service of
the Boston Public Library. After
serving for about three years as
Curator of Pamphlets and Periodicals
and Keeper of the Prince and Barton
Libraries, and during this time preparing, in connection with Mr. J. M.
Hubbard, a Shakespearian Catalogue
which was highly commended, he
was appointed Librarian of Bates
Hall, and held this responsible position until his last illness, a period of
more than twenty years. Here he
found his life work, and in this employment his life was spent happily
and in the highest sense of the word
successfully. His life must have
been happy, because his modest ambitions were satisfied, his tasks were
such as were best suited to his tastes
and talents, and he must have
enjoyed the consciousness that he
had won the esteem and friendship
of those with whom he was brought
into pleasant relations in the per-

formance of his daily duties. His life was truly successful, because it was spent in a constant succession of acts of service to others, and in rendering these services, his own stores of knowledge were increased, his mind was expanded and strengthened, and his character became riper and sweeter. Although he lived among books, he was in no sense a recluse. It was his duty as Librarian of Bates Hall to place his knowledge of the treasures of the Library at the disposal of every applicant needing his help or guidance, and it was said that "almost no other individual in the city was in personal contact with so many people as was Mr. Knapp." In this trying position his patience and courtesy never failed, and so retentive was his memory, so thorough his acquaintance with the contents of the Library, and so general and exact his knowledge upon a vast variety of subjects, that he rarely failed to supply the information needed. The many tributes which appeared in the press after his death uniformly testified to the admirable manner in which his duties were performed and to the spirit of Christian courtesy which he displayed to persons of all characters, often under circumstances which must have been very trying to his equanimity. These tributes also show how widely he was known as a scholar and as an accomplished librarian, and how universally he was esteemed and admired by the many frequenters of the Library.

His faithfulness to his duties was unswerving, while the most hasty visitor could not fail to note that the Library in which he was so important a factor, was his pride and delight. His record is one of a life well spent in useful and honorable work, of fidelity to principle, and of native talents developed and strengthened by cultivation and worthy use. We, his classmates, shall miss him on our visits to the Public Library, at Commencements, which he frequently attended, and in the social gatherings of the class, while to his associates in his work and to the many students who looked to him for advice and assistance, the loss is almost irreparable.

Extracts from Official Documents of the Boston Public Library.

From the Annual Report of the Trustees, February 1, 1899:—

The Library has suffered by the deaths and resignations of some of those employed in its service.

The most conspicuous loss was occasioned by the death of Mr. Arthur Mason Knapp, who was twenty-four years in its service, and for twenty years the Custodian of Bates Hall. His experience, ability, and fidelity were universally acknowledged, and possessed an added charm by reason of his agreeable personal traits.

From the Librarian's Annual Report, February 1, 1899, signed Herbert Putnam:—

The Library has suffered serious loss by death. Most serious indeed was the loss of Arthur Mason

Knapp, for twenty-four years in its service, and for the last twenty years its chief reference librarian as Custodian of Bates Hall. Mr. Knapp's accumulated experience in the work of this position, to which he devoted himself with absolute concentration, stood for an asset of exceeding value. Rather than minute here too briefly the record of his career and service, I append to be printed the notice published in the Bulletin after his death, and passages from the address of the Rev. Dr. James DeNormandie (who as a member of the Library Board spoke with particular knowledge) at the funeral services.

From the Monthly Bulletin, January, 1899 :—

ARTHUR MASON KNAPP.

1839–1898.

On Tuesday, December 27, 1898, died Arthur Mason Knapp, Custodian of Bates Hall in the Boston Public Library.

He was born at St. Johnsbury,

Vermont, August 8, 1839, the son of
Hiram Knapp and Sophronia Brown.
During his boyhood the family removed to Boston, where he fitted for
college at the Boston Latin School.
He was graduated as the first scholar
in his class, and entered Harvard
College as a member of the class of
1863. He held from Harvard the
degree of A.M. as well as that of
A.B.

After teaching for some years in
Phillips Academy, Andover, in the
Boston Latin School, and in the
Brookline High School, he entered
the service of the Library January
23, 1875. His first appointment was
to the charge of the special collections of the Library; from 1878
until his death he held the position
of Custodian of Bates Hall.

His knowledge of Shakespeariana
and of Elizabethan literature was of
great value in the preparation of the
catalogue of the Barton collection.
In his position in charge of the main
reference department of the Library,

his special knowledge of the subject of genealogy and local history, as well as a thorough general knowledge of the resources of the Library on all subjects, was of the greatest service to an immense constituency of readers. To the value of this service, rendered with exact conscientiousness and singleness of purpose in its relation to his colleagues, and with assiduity and personal interest towards the readers and students who came to him for assistance, the warm appreciation of all those with whom he came in contact bears witness.

EXTRACTS FROM PERSONAL LETTERS

*Relating to His Work as Librarian
and as Teacher.*

———

"To me it was a delight to deal with a librarian who never offered his views or preferences to my studies, who permitted me always to brush conventional books aside, and quickly understood the pursuit of sound evidence. He had no fads. He could laugh at the credulity of genealogists, whose books he knew better than most librarians. He was a good American and New Englander, yet not parochial. I have no doubt that he was profoundly religious, as no man would have the truthfulness, the courage, the modesty, the patient service of others, the unselfishness, that marked him, but a mind steeped in devoutness and sustained by faith."

"We shall never go to the Library

without a thought of him. He was so invariably kind and patient and so helpful that no one can ever take just his place."

"In all the professional work I tried to do in Boston, I was helped more by him to find what I needed than by any one else; and for that assistance, rendered in his own quiet way, I have always been very grateful."

"I am but one among the many who have grateful, loving thoughts for courtesy and help and kindness, always so freely bestowed, from my early Latin School days on through college and master's degree work."

"Mr. Knapp's going out from his field of work affected me — to him a stranger — very deeply, so valuable had been his assistance to me from time to time, so gentle and patient and kindly was he with every bothering request. I never felt at home in

Bates Hall till he took the chair in the new building, within the reach of every one — the scholar and the gentleman — to unlock those stores of learning. How deep my debt to him! How gracious his memory!"

From a letter addressed to Mr. George B. Knapp, by Rev. Edward T. Fairbanks, D.D., of St. Johnsbury, Vt.:—

I think of the happy morning when you and I stood in the gallery of Bates Hall and saw him going down with the books to Miss T. It is delightful to have that Hall and Public Library linked in my thought with the little fellow whose young life in Fairbanks Village rounded up into so much dignity and responsibility in one of the great city institutions. I think it was a good providence that brought Arthur Knapp, notwithstanding his modest and retiring disposition, up into the place where his excelling worth and abilities could find scope and become appreciated. His life seems to me rare and beautiful. We had a short, happy call from him when he was last here. I always expected to see him sometime during the summer or fall as surely as I expected the corn to tassel or the maple orchards to hang out their red banners. These hills and groves were a fresh joy to him every time he came. Dear fellow! He was lovable and goodly, strong and true. It pains me to think of you with Arthur no more at your side. Your tastes and his were almost identical, and I know you each appreciated that double kinship. And, in fact, will right along. It is a blessed fact that traits, and loves, are not changed by this translation. And one day the threads will be gathered up again and minds and hearts go on together as aforetime — together up higher paths.

From Prof. Benjamin W. Wells, of the University of the South, at Sewanee, Tenn.:—

I was both a public and a private pupil of your brother, and was very

much attached to him in my boyhood, and he has ever since been
connected with the pleasantest memories of my school life.

I recall particularly his teaching
in Latin and in physics. There was
a little air of gloom about his room
[in the old Brookline High School],
especially as compared with Miss
Bartlett's beyond, but we found little
time to think of that when his teaching once began.

Mr. Knapp was an excellent
teacher, careful, precise, rather strict,
and inflexibly just. [Here follows
the story of an attempted annoyance,
which the teacher bore with such
unruffled temper that the pupils were
shamed into propriety.]

I think what impressed us all
most in Mr. Knapp was his genuine
interest in us, as school boys and
girls, and afterwards. He never for-
got one of his pupils. I have often
asked him in later years about old
school acquaintances who to me were
only names. He seemed to have

followed them all with affectionate solicitude, and I am sure they all could count on his sympathy in every success and disappointment.

From Miss Marion McGregor Noyes, Instructor in Philosophy in Colorado College :—

My sense of personal loss in the death of your brother is very great. For many years I have depended upon his friendship and interest, and in returning to Boston have sought him out in the Library, sure of such a welcome as dwells ever in one's memory. . . .

I find it difficult to describe the unusual element in Mr. Knapp's teaching — for unusual it was. Perhaps were I to say that we felt that we were each *two persons* to him, this would in some degree express my meaning. He valued faithful work and accurate scholarship very highly, and there was great satisfaction in winning his word of commendation. But we knew that he was so much interested in us personally, that even if we were indifferent or lazy, he would have patience with us and would *continue to like us* (provided, of course, we had once won his esteem). He made us all feel his interest in us and his ambition for us. And yet I cannot recall that he ever expressed any such sentiments in words. It was all given in that subtle, quiet way which made his personal relations so unique. . . .

We were fond of spending our recess with him, and his desk was generally surrounded at this time. His reserve was so great that we felt it a rare privilege when he opened to us the treasure house of his mind, as he was always ready to do when he found us ready to listen. In short, we honored him and loved him.

He was at one time suffering much from lameness, being obliged to use crutches. His patience under very evident suffering impressed us deeply. It was my privilege to walk with him from the horse-car to the school quite often, and I used to enjoy these times very greatly. He

would talk about his interests or
ours, as the case might be, but
always with an alertness of mind
and of sympathy which has not been
forgotten, I am sure, by any of those
pupils who could then, or later, count
themselves as among his friends.

His sense of humor we always
counted upon, and we watched for
the smile, which he tried in vain to
conceal, when one in our class who
had the gift of being very amusing
—albeit not always at the right
time — was exerting his powers. It
was difficult for Mr. Knapp to be
severe under these circumstances,
and we knew it.

He taught us to reverence a high
standard of work. I think that,
more than any teacher I have ever
had, he taught us the meaning of the
word *faithfulness* — not only to a
high ideal, but to our own native
powers, whether great or little.
This and his unfailing and sponta-
neous courtesy seemed to me the
central points in his character.

TRIBUTES FROM THE PRESS.

From the Boston Herald :—

Arthur Mason Knapp, for twenty years Librarian of Bates Hall, in the Boston Public Library, and in charge during that period of the main card catalogue, died Tuesday at his home, 52 Montgomery Street. He was stricken with paralysis early in the month.

He was a graduate of Harvard, class of '63, and was a classmate of the late ex-Governor Greenhalge, John Fiske, the historian ; ex-Secretary of the Treasury, C. S. Fairchild, and F. L. Higginson. He was born in St. Johnsbury, Vt., August 8, 1839, and prepared for college in the Boston Latin School. After leaving Harvard he taught the classics and mathematics at Phillips Andover Academy and at the Brookline High School.

On January 23, 1875, he joined the Public Library staff, at first as Curator of Periodicals and Pamphlets, beside what are called the "cabinet" books in the Barton and Prince Libraries — large folios in curious and rare bindings, dear to the bibliophile. He catalogued the Barton Library of Shakespeariana, and acquired in the work a taste for research in Shakespeare's doings that endured to his death. He was married in 1873 to Miss Abbie Bartlett, who died in 1876.

In 1878 he was placed in charge of Bates Hall, and became probably the best known personage to the general public around the Library. He was a target for all sorts of questions on every conceivable subject, and was rarely at loss for a satisfactory response. He united a patient and courteous manner, a gift for research and a knowledge of the resources of the great library, that made him an invaluable aid to the student anxious to explore its riches.

His place developed a unique variety of talent, which could perhaps be generalized as a knowledge of books, though he sedulously avoided a desultory habit by thoroughly working up a few specialties. He became a profound student of early Elizabethan literature, largely as one result of his studies in Shakespeare. He had always kept up in genealogy long before it had attained its present vogue, and was one of the recognized authorities in that curious field of research.

Aside from these subjects, he had of necessity some sort of information in almost every branch of knowledge, and in very many had a great deal, the countless questions showered upon him in his daily work compelling a delving in both familiar and out-of-the-way lines. Authors working up a "period" in their work, students looking for a clew to the latest in their branches, stage people seeking points on costume, artists searching for historical "motifs," are samples of the varied sort of people he had to meet, all of whom were set agoing satisfactorily, and, if time served, were often buried in an embarrassment of riches.

The funeral services will be held at two o'clock to-morrow afternoon at the Shawmut Church, corner of Tremont and West Brookline Streets.

From the Boston Evening Transcript : —

Mr. Arthur Mason Knapp, Custodian of Bates Hall of the Boston Public Library, died at his home Tuesday afternoon after a short illness. These tidings will bring sorrow to many who have known him or sought his help at the Library. Mr. Knapp, the son of Hiram and Sophronia (Brown) Knapp, was born at St. Johnsbury, Vt., August 8, 1839. During his boyhood his family removed to Boston, where he fitted for college at the Boston Latin School. He was graduated from there as the first scholar in his class and entered

Harvard College as a member of the class of 1863. He held from Harvard the degree of A.M. as well as that of A.B.

After a few years spent in teaching in Phillips (Andover) Academy and the Brookline High School he entered the service of the Boston Public Library January 23, 1875. He was at first placed in charge of the special collections of the Library, and later appointed Custodian of Bates Hall.

With absolute devotion he gave to the discharge of the duties of his office an unintermittent service of nearly twenty-four years. To the value of those services, rendered with intense conscientiousness and genuine interest, all who have had occasion to use the Boston Public Library can bear witness.

His knowledge of Shakespeariana and Elizabethan literature was special and thorough, and greatly serviceable in the preparation of the catalogue of the Barton collection, while the general knowledge of the Library gained by him in the interpretation of its resources during twenty years' conduct of the chief reference department of the Library was of immense avail to a large constituency of readers.

Mr. Knapp married July 2, 1873, Miss Abbie Bartlett, daughter of the late James Bartlett of Brookline; she died January 26, 1876. Since her death he has lived in this city with his widowed mother and his sister, who, with a brother, survive him. He was a member of Shawmut Congregational Church, to which he was a generous giver. His funeral will be from that church on Friday afternoon at two o'clock. Rev. William E. Barton will officiate at the services, and among the pall-bearers will be Herbert Putnam, James L. Whitney, and Lindsay Swift of the Public Library. In the hallway of the Library building has been placed a large wreath, tied with a black ribbon, and bearing an inscription in memory of Mr. Knapp.

From the Boston Journal, omitting facts previously given :—

Mr. Knapp's official title was Custodian of Bates Hall. He it was to whom would-be readers or investigators turned for information and help in selecting material for reference or reading. It was his business to know what was at hand and to help persons to it. And in his quiet way he did much to aid many. Probably no one in the Library was more universally liked than was he, and that not only by the public, but by the employees as well. This is shown by the number of communications that have poured in to the Librarian from many persons that had known Mr. Knapp, either as readers or as former employees of the Library, who hasten thus to express sorrow for the loss of such a helper, and to testify to his worth.

He was graduated from Harvard College in 1863.

From The Congregationalist:—

A PUBLIC SERVANT.

Arthur Mason Knapp, who died December 27, had probably rendered as definite and helpful services to the citizens of Boston in general during the last twenty years as any of his contemporaries. His position in the Public Library, where he had charge of Bates Hall and the card catalogue, brought hosts of people to him to make inquiries concerning serviceable literature. His remarkable knowledge of books, as well as his fund of information on all sorts of subjects, made him an invaluable counselor, while his quiet, even manner left its impress upon all who came in contact with him. In the life of Shawmut Church, which he had attended for many years, he filled his own peculiar and important place.

From the Boston Pilot:—

In recording the death of Mr. Arthur M. Knapp, Custodian and Librarian in Bates Hall of the Boston Public Library, which occurred on Tuesday, December 27, 1898, the *Pilot* desires to add its tribute to that of the general expression of regret at the public loss at his demise. For Mr. Knapp's scholarly attributes, general fund of information, and un-varying urbanity and readiness to put that information at the disposal of all, the *Pilot* is at one with the cordial acknowledgment in these regards, of the myriads who had the pleasure of Mr. Knapp's friendship. It is no underrating of his successor to hope that even at a long distance he may be able to follow such an amiable public official.

From Time and the Hour : —

Mr. Knapp will be missed by the old *habitués* of the Public Library more than any other officer there, since he was for so many years the "man at the front" during the day-time. He enjoyed the best sort of popularity, won by courtesy, urban-ity, and evenness of temper. He was unassuming in bearing, but no man was more competent than he in his calling. His service as Custodian of Bates Hall, covering nearly a quarter of a century, had made him a master of his particular art. He was a Harvard man, graduating in a class which embraced a number of men who have become conspicuous in their professions and trades here in Boston, among them Charles P. Bowditch, Francis C. Loring, Dr. George B. Shattuck, James Brown, the publisher, Andrew J. Bailey, our city solicitor, Dr. John C. Warren, Henry N. Sheldon, George B. Chase. Beginning his career as a tutor and then a schoolmaster, first in Phillips (Andover) Academy, then in Brookline, and for a short time in the Boston Latin School, where he had been prepared for college, he entered the Public Library service in his young manhood, so that the best of his life has been devoted to it. He has left his mark as the compiler of the Barton Library catalogue, of a catalogue of family histories, of the index to the portraits in the Thayer collection, the list of portraits of Franklin owned by the Library, and of sundry other useful works. He was a lover of books and an intelligent collector, interested especially in illuminated manuscripts, of which he possessed a choice collection. He also found pleasure and some profit in collecting coins and medals. He was a good citizen, faithful to every duty, and went his quiet way evenly and without reproach. Who could ask a better epitaph?

From the Bangor Saturday Commercial : —

The editor of this department of the *Saturday Commercial* feels a keen personal loss in the death of Mr. Arthur M. Knapp, Custodian of Bates Hall, of the Boston Public Library. While preparing a work upon an entirely new and somewhat difficult subject which was published in New York in 1894, we had occasion to spend a considerable time in searching authorities and out-of-the-way books in that magnificent reference library. This work extended over a considerable time for two years, at intervals, during which we had our separate working table with just as many volumes at a time as were wanted. Mr. Knapp was constant and kindly in his attentions, always ready to assist, to offer suggestions, and put us on the track of information. Our books were left just where we stopped work at night and were ready for us in the morning, with Mr. Knapp's gentle and helpful ways to assist in the day's work. It was a pleasure to make public acknowledgment of Mr. Knapp's aid in the introduction to that work, and to present a copy to the Bates Hall shelves as a further acknowledgment of our indebtedness to that magnificent Library.

THE WORLD BEAUTIFUL.

In the way of a faithful and noble life, which gave itself with the rarest self-abnegation, patience, and gentleness to the service of each and all, that of Arthur Mason Knapp, Curator of Bates Hall in the Public Library, may well be held in reverence and forever enshrined in the World Beautiful. A personality so delicately unobtrusive, so swift in sympathetic response, and so generous in its aid to every seeker, came to be, to the multitude of students and visitors in the Library, almost as the air or the sunlight, and only when it is forever vanished from our sight do we realize how in Mr. Knapp were embodied those high qualities which the followers of the divine life may well pause to consider. There was almost no other individual in the city who was in personal contact with so many people as was Mr. Knapp. Daily, for twenty-three years, he had directed the most important and most populous department of the Library. An *habitué* of Bates Hall could not but take into his life the lesson of the patience, the gentleness, the flawless courtesy that characterized Mr. Knapp. His presence had a benignant character that seemed to radiate a certain serene uplifting. Frivolity shrank abashed from the atmosphere of simple, earnest, scholarly activity with which he invested the departmental work. His unvarying courtesy tacitly compelled or rather inspired courtesy in others. To the learned or the ignorant, the loftiest or the lowliest, he was always the same simple, considerate, gracious gentleman. If a manner so unconscious and unobtrusive as his could invite characterization, it would suggest the ethics as expressed by Hamlet to Polonius. "My lord," said Polonius, "I will use them according to their deserts." But the Prince replied, "No; use them after your own honor and dignity." These words perfectly describe the manner of the learned and beloved Curator — that of treating every person according to his own high standard of honor and dignity. Nor in thus dwelling for a moment on his manner is there emphasized a mere incidental matter devoid of significance. Manners are not only as important as morals, but to a great degree are the expression, the register that indicates the degree of moral achievement. As Tennyson well says : —

"For manners are not idle, but the fruit
Of loyal nature and of noble mind."

In such an office as that held by Mr. Knapp the manner and the personal presence were most significant factors. Here there were pouring in hundreds of persons each day, comprising all classes, and including many visitors from afar, as well as the residents of the city. From nearly each one of all the vast and varying throng were made continual demands upon the Curator. The information, advice, or directions asked of him were of the widest range, and his treasures of learning, his specific knowledge of books, his wise suggestions were generously given. To each and all he gave freely of his best. The only limitation was in the receptivity of the inquirer, not with the knowledge he imparted or the counsel he gave. The nervous strain of turning the mind to a different subject a dozen times an hour; of directing the inquirer to certain places for books, or of going himself in pursuit of rare volumes, as he so frequently and constantly did — the nervous tax of such work is beyond computation. Yet never was there the slightest irritation or impatience on his part. Always was he the same patient, considerate, generous, and courteous gentleman. He spent his life and his time in those high pursuits and in that state of mental and moral aspiration that allowed the spirit to evolve, and he lived, while here, the spiritual life. In a most vital way was he "the friend and aider of all who would live in the spirit." The literal manner in which one may seek, first, the kingdom of God and his righteousness is to fulfill one's duties. . . .

Knowledge changes into character, and how greatly then does one who so wisely guides multitudes to knowledge as did Mr. Knapp influence and help to predetermine the general character of the community. The spacious interior of our noble Library could not have contained the wreaths if each one, whose life has been enlarged and uplifted by Mr. Knapp, had brought there his tribute.

"Without me, ye can do nothing." No one more truly felt the inner reliance of these words than our friend, whose life was so pure and faithful a following of the Christ. What can be said more than that he was a Christian gentleman; one whose character it is good to dwell

113

upon in setting out on the pilgrimage of the new year. He was a faithful servant of Christ. He fed his life constantly from the divine springs, and he *lived* his religion. When some of those to whom his work was sacred and his presence dear gathered to pay the last earthly tribute, the keynote of the beautiful words by his pastor, Rev. Dr. Barton, and by Rev. Dr. DeNormandie, as one of the trustees of the Library — the keynote of the expression was that he was faithful. The simple expression holds untold significance. To be faithful in life — this may well be the aspiration and the purpose of every heart.

The new year is the festival of faith. It is the annual covenant between the soul and God. With the high ideal of a life of faith shall ever be linked the name of him who invested the aspiration with new and noble possibilities of fulfillment — Arthur Mason Knapp.

114

Oscar Fay Adams, in Boston Evening Transcript, December 30 : —

ARTHUR MASON KNAPP
1839–1898.

Now when they came to look upon the face of him who had died ere he had come to threescore years, there were some who would fain have lamented sore, and beat the breast by reason of their sorrow, for they had loved him much. And then it was as if a bright mist was suddenly spread about them and their grief was stilled, while from out of the mist-cloud came, as it were, voices, but very sweet, such as none had ever before heard their like. And the voices made, as it might be, speech with one another, and the matter of their speech was all of what he had done for each of them, who himself had now with time no more to do. And the voices had ever their one tale to tell, the tale of help from him, and moreover of how he had counted not himself of any worth soever, but only so as he might serve those who ever came to him daily. And there were innumerable of these voices, and they made sweet melody together that day. And presently their fair, sweet speech with one another came to an end, and there were heard yet other voices chanting, so as it were, a great way off, but of their chanting might those who stood within the bright mist-cloud hear only the one word "faithful," but none other clearly. And when these voices had made an end in their turn, and their melody was quite departed, they who had listened were fain to go their ways and were not a little comforted among themselves by reason of the melody that had reached their ears that day.